My

A humorous
rhyming story

First published in 2006 by
Franklin Watts
338 Euston Road
London
NW1 3BH

Franklin Watts Australia
Hachette Children's Books
Level 17/207 Kent Street
Sydney
NSW 2000

A CIP catalogue record for this book is available
from the British Library.

ISBN 0 7496 6547 5 (hbk)
ISBN 0 7496 6554 8 (pbk)

Series Editor: Jackie Hamley
Series Advisors: Dr Barrie Wade, Dr Hilary Minns
Design: Peter Scoulding

Printed in China

READING CORNER

My Nan

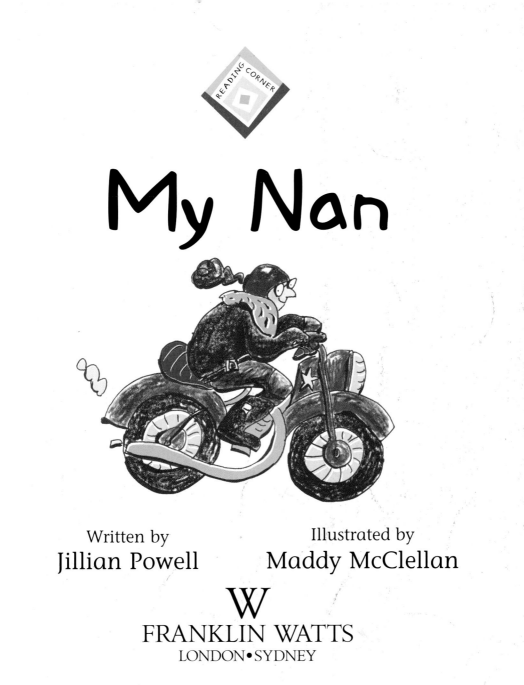

Written by
Jillian Powell

Illustrated by
Maddy McClellan

W
FRANKLIN WATTS
LONDON • SYDNEY

Jillian Powell

"My nana had auburn hair and wore earrings like blackberries. I can still remember jumping up with excitement when she came to visit."

Maddy McClellan

"My nan lived on the other side of the world so I hardly ever got to see her. The only thing I really remember is that she liked marzipan covered in chocolate!"

My nan is not like other nans.

She eats hot dogs and drinks from cans.

She does things that annoy my mum –

– like blowing bright-pink bubble gum.

While other nans knit
socks and jumpers,
my nan likes to
drive big dumpers.

Some nans dress up in gloves and suits.
Mine wears hard hats and welly boots.

Other nans have dogs or cats,
but my nan has fifteen pet rats!

Some nans teach budgies how to talk –
mine takes her rats out for a walk.

Most nans like gentle sports like bowls.

My nan is out there scoring goals.

When you're at your nan's for tea,

do you have such fun as me?

Your nan can surely bake a cake,
but mine knows how to charm
a snake.

Some nans go to evening classes,
catch the bus with cheap bus passes.

16

But my nan says
the bus is slow.
Her motorbike can really go!

When your nan takes you to the park,
she gets you home before it's dark.

She helps you reach the monkey rings
and doesn't stay out on the swings.

Some nans have hobbies like
brass-rubbing.

But my nan likes to go out clubbing.

She loves the music really loud,
and lets her hair down in a crowd.

When other nans sit down to rest,
mine goes to take her flying test.

She loops the loop and spins around while we stand watching from the ground.

Your nan may give you simple treats like lollipops and bags of sweets.

She takes you shopping in the sales,
while mine takes me out
watching whales!

While other nans are watching soaps,
my nan is learning to climb ropes.

Some nans have problems
with their knees,
but my nan swings
from a trapeze.

No other nans are like my nan –
they can't do half the things she can.
But I would never swap my nan,
because ...

... I am her biggest fan!

Notes for parents and teachers

READING CORNER has been structured to provide maximum support for new readers. The stories may be used by adults for sharing with young children. Primarily, however, the stories are designed for newly independent readers, whether they are reading these books in bed at night, or in the reading corner at school or in the library.

Starting to read alone can be a daunting prospect. READING CORNER helps by providing visual support and repeating words and phrases, while making reading enjoyable. These books will develop confidence in the new reader, and encourage a love of reading that will last a lifetime!

If you are reading this book with a child, here are a few tips:

1. Make reading fun! Choose a time to read when you and the child are relaxed and have time to share the story.

2. Encourage children to reread the story, and to retell the story in their own words, using the illustrations to remind them what has happened.

3. Give praise! Remember that small mistakes need not always be corrected.

READING CORNER covers three grades of early reading ability, with three levels at each grade. Each level has a certain number of words per story, indicated by the number of bars on the spine of the book, to allow you to choose the right book for a young reader:

GRADE 1	GRADE 2	GRADE 3
50 words	130 words	250 words
70 words	160 words	350 words
100 words	200 words	450 words